Serendipity in the Stacks

Serendipity in the Stacks

MOSES MUTISO

Published by MOSES MUTISO, 2024.

This is a work of fiction. Similarities to real people, places, or events are entirely coincidental.

SERENDIPITY IN THE STACKS

First edition. December 11, 2024.

ISBN: 979-8230491507

Written by MOSES MUTISO.

Also by MOSES MUTISO

Embrace Your Size: A Guide to Managing Body Image and Health
The Fall from Grace: A Story of Manipulation in a Mega Church
Behind the Veil of Control The Tactics of Dark Lords
Beyond the Screen A Journey Toward Conscious Living
Embrace Your Size: A Guide to Managing Body Image and Health
Serendipity in the Stacks
Serendipity in the Stacks
Serendipity in the Stacks

Introduction

Chapter 1: The Rainy Day Encounter

- Lila's background: her career as a journalist, her burnout, and why she retreats to bookstores.
- Ethan's life as an architect, his introverted nature, and his love for design and books.
- Their first encounter at the indie bookstore: the playful banter over the book they both reach for.
- A fleeting yet magnetic conversation before they part ways, neither asking for contact information.

Chapter 2: Crossing Paths

- Lila's busy week and how she keeps replaying the conversation in her head.
- Ethan's creative frustrations at work, interspersed with thoughts of the "bookstore girl."
- A chance meeting at a subway station, where they chat briefly and exchange first names.
- Growing curiosity and attraction, but still, no exchange of numbers.

Chapter 3: Digital Dating Woes

- Lila's friend convinces her to try a dating app, leading to a string of disastrous (and funny) dates.
- Ethan's colleagues set him up with someone who's the opposite of what he's looking for.
- Both reflect on the challenges of finding meaningful connections in a digital age.
- A moment of serendipity when they bump into each other at a local coffee shop, leading to an extended conversation.

Chapter 4: Building a Connection

- Their first planned outing: a quirky, unconventional date at an art exhibit.
- Conversations that reveal their shared love for literature, art, and wanderlust.
- Lila's hesitation to let her guard down due to a past breakup.
- Ethan's quiet determination to show her he's different.

Chapter 5: Conflicts and Missteps

- Lila receives a major career opportunity that requires her full attention.
- Ethan learns he must temporarily relocate for a high-profile project.
- Miscommunications arise when Lila feels Ethan is pulling away, while Ethan thinks Lila is too focused on her career.
- A heated argument where insecurities surface, leaving both wondering if they're meant to be.

Chapter 6: The Distance Between Us

- Lila's inner struggle: balancing her desire for independence with her feelings for Ethan.
- Ethan's life in his new city, missing Lila but unsure how to reach out.
- The impact of their separation: both characters reflect on their past relationships and what they truly want from love.
- Heartfelt advice from friends or family that helps them gain clarity.

Chapter 7: Small Steps Toward Reconciliation

- Lila sends Ethan a care package, including a book that reminds her of their first meeting.
- Ethan surprises Lila with a spontaneous visit, showing vulnerability and commitment.
- They agree to take things slow, focusing on honest communication.

Chapter 8: The Grand Gesture

- Ethan completes his project and returns to New York, surprising Lila at the bookstore where they first met.
- A heartfelt conversation where they acknowledge their fears and hopes for the future.
- Ethan's "grand gesture," such as designing a small, cozy reading nook for Lila in her apartment.

Chapter 9: Love in the Real World

- The challenges of integrating their lives while maintaining individuality.
- Lila's decision to set boundaries at work to prioritize her personal life.
- Ethan's rediscovery of his passion for architecture, influenced by Lila's creative spirit.
- Celebrating their growth as a couple through small, everyday moments.

Epilogue: A Future Together

- A few years later, Lila and Ethan are thriving both individually and as a couple.
- They reflect on how their chance encounter transformed their lives.
- Closing the story with a sweet moment that mirrors their first meeting, like browsing books together in the same store.

Introduction: The Symphony of Serendipity

Lila Andrews clutched her coffee cup like a lifeline as she stepped into the small, independent bookstore. The rain outside painted the city in a palette of muted grays, its rhythmic patter a stark contrast to the vibrant coziness within. Shelves crammed with books towered like guardians of forgotten worlds, their spines whispering promises of escape and adventure.

The smell of aged paper and freshly brewed coffee wrapped around her like a familiar hug, soothing the frazzled edges of her mind. It had been weeks since she'd allowed herself a moment of reprieve from the whirlwind of deadlines and newsroom chaos that defined her life. And here, amidst the comforting disorder of mismatched shelves and creaky wooden floors, she finally felt a semblance of peace.

She wandered aimlessly, running her fingers along the spines of books, her thoughts a jumbled mess of story pitches, unanswered emails, and a nagging sense of discontent. Her career as a journalist had once been a dream, a fire that burned brightly in her twenties. But now, at twenty-eight, the flames had dulled to embers, buried beneath the suffocating weight of expectations and exhaustion.

In the far corner of the store, she found herself in the classics section. Titles by Austen, Brontë, and Tolstoy lined the shelves, their timelessness a stark reminder of her own fleeting existence. She reached out for a weathered copy of Pride and Prejudice, only to find her hand colliding with another's.

"Sorry," a deep voice said, his tone warm yet hesitant.

Lila looked up, her gaze meeting a pair of strikingly blue eyes framed by wire-rimmed glasses. The man smiled, his hand retracting awkwardly.

"You first," he added, gesturing to the book.

"No, no, it's fine," Lila replied, a small smile tugging at her lips. "I was just... browsing."

"Me too." He chuckled, a sound that was as unassuming as it was pleasant. "Though I guess it's a bit cliché, isn't it? Two strangers reaching for Pride and Prejudice on a rainy day in a bookstore."

Lila laughed softly, surprised at how easily the tension melted away. "I suppose it is. But I think Austen would approve. She did have a thing for serendipitous encounters."

They stood there for a moment, the world around them fading into the background. Lila noticed the faint hint of rain lingering on his coat, the way his glasses fogged slightly from the warmth of the store. He seemed out of place, yet entirely at home—like a misplaced bookmark in a cherished novel.

"I'm Ethan, by the way," he said, offering his hand.

"Lila," she replied, shaking it briefly.

Ethan glanced at the book in her hand and smiled. "Austen fan?"

"More like a serial re-reader," Lila admitted. "I've lost count of how many times I've read this one. There's just something comforting about returning to it."

"I get that," Ethan said. "Books have a way of grounding us, don't they? Like anchors in the chaos."

Lila tilted her head, intrigued by his choice of words. "An architect with a poetic soul. That's a rare combination."

Ethan chuckled again, this time with a hint of self-consciousness. "And a journalist with a penchant for classics. Also rare."

Their conversation flowed effortlessly, a dance of words and laughter that felt both natural and unexpected. They talked about favorite authors, debated the merits of various genres, and discovered a shared love for indie bookstores. It was a conversation that could have lasted hours, but reality had other plans.

The sound of a phone alarm interrupted them, its sharp beep cutting through the warm ambience.

"That's my cue," Ethan said, a note of regret in his voice. "I have to get back to work."

Lila nodded, feeling an inexplicable pang of disappointment. "It was nice meeting you, Ethan."

"Likewise," he replied. "Maybe I'll see you around."

And just like that, he was gone, leaving Lila standing alone in the classics section, clutching the book they'd both reached for.

As Lila left the bookstore, the rain had softened into a misty drizzle. She pulled her coat tighter around her and stepped onto the slick pavement, the memory of Ethan's easy smile lingering in her mind. She wasn't sure why she felt so drawn to him. Maybe it was his calm demeanor, a striking contrast to the whirlwind of people she usually encountered in her profession. Or maybe it was the way he'd looked at her—like he genuinely wanted to hear what she had to say.

It was rare to meet someone who felt so... effortless. Most interactions in her world were transactional—networking over drinks, interviews where every word was calculated, even friendships that often revolved around mutual convenience. Ethan, in just a few minutes, had managed to cut through all of that.

But Lila wasn't one to indulge in fantasies, not anymore. Life had taught her that serendipity wasn't a guarantee; it was a fleeting moment, like catching a firefly in the dark. She had learned to rely on herself, to focus on what she could control. And yet, as she stood at the corner waiting for the light to change, she couldn't help but wonder: What if I see him again?

Across the city, Ethan adjusted his glasses and glanced at the clock on his desk. He was late, as usual, but for once, he didn't mind. His thoughts were still in that little bookstore, replaying snippets of his conversation with Lila.

She had an energy about her—sharp yet approachable, like she could disarm you with a single witty comment but still make you feel entirely at ease. He couldn't remember the last time he'd felt so connected to someone so quickly. His life rarely left room for such connections.

As an architect, Ethan's days were consumed by blueprints and client meetings, his evenings spent in quiet solitude with a book or sketchpad. It wasn't that he disliked his life—he found genuine joy in his work and his creative pursuits—but it often felt... predictable. Safe.

Meeting Lila had been anything but predictable. He didn't even know her last name, yet he felt like he'd known her for years. He found himself wondering what it would be like to see her again, to learn more about the stories behind her confident smile and thoughtful gaze.

But he quickly pushed the thought aside. Life didn't work like that. He'd had his fair share of disappointments to know that much. Relationships, he'd learned, were messy and complicated. He wasn't sure he was ready for that again.

Still, as he leaned back in his chair and stared out the window at the rain-soaked city, he couldn't shake the feeling that something had shifted.

Lila's week unfolded in its usual chaotic fashion—morning editorial meetings, hurried lunches at her desk, late nights chasing stories. But in quiet moments, her mind wandered back to Ethan. She caught herself scanning the subway crowd during her commute, lingering a little longer in the bookstore on Saturday, and even looking up at the high-rise buildings downtown, wondering if one of them housed his office.

It was silly, she told herself. New York was a city of millions. The odds of seeing him again were slim. And yet, wasn't it the unexpected moments that made life interesting?

On Sunday, Lila met her best friend, Marissa, for brunch at their usual spot. Over mimosas and avocado toast, Marissa listened with growing amusement as Lila recounted the bookstore encounter.

"You're smitten," Marissa teased, raising an eyebrow.

"I am not," Lila shot back, though the warmth in her cheeks betrayed her.

"Oh, please. You've spent the past ten minutes talking about his eyes. You didn't even know his last name!"

"Exactly," Lila said, folding her arms. "Which is why it's pointless to think about him. It's not like I'm going to run into him again."

"Maybe not," Marissa conceded, "but if you do, you'd better get his number this time."

Lila laughed, but her friend's words lingered. She hadn't felt this way about someone in a long time—if ever. And though she wasn't sure she believed in fate, she couldn't deny the flicker of hope in her chest.

For Ethan, life continued in its usual rhythm, punctuated by client calls and late-night design sessions. But every so often, he caught himself thinking about Lila. He even found himself back at the bookstore one evening, wandering through the aisles as if she might appear.

He told himself it was ridiculous. He didn't even know her last name, let alone how to find her. But the memory of her laughter, the way her eyes lit up when she talked about books, stayed with him.

One night, after a particularly frustrating day at work, Ethan found himself sketching. It was something he often did to unwind, his pencil moving instinctively across the page. When he finally looked down at his work, he realized he'd drawn the interior of the bookstore, complete with a figure standing in the classics section.

He shook his head, laughing softly at himself. "Get a grip, Ethan," he muttered, setting the sketchpad aside. But even as he tried to focus on something else, a quiet voice in the back of his mind whispered: What if?

Chapter 2: Crossing Paths

Lila's Busy Week

The week after the chance encounter at the bookstore was a whirlwind for Lila Carter. As a junior editor at Harper & Wilde Publishing, deadlines loomed like storm clouds, each manuscript demanding her attention with a ferocity she couldn't ignore. She worked late every night, her desk a chaos of sticky notes, coffee mugs, and printouts marked in red ink. Yet, amidst the chaos, one moment kept intruding on her thoughts—the conversation with the man who had appeared like an unexpected chapter in her own life.

Lila sat at her desk, staring at her monitor, but the words on the screen blurred into irrelevance. Instead, her mind replayed his voice, low and warm, like the bass notes of a favorite song. He had seemed genuinely curious, asking her opinion about the book he'd picked up—a rare memoir about a painter who had lived an extraordinary but troubled life. She had noticed his eyes, sharp and intelligent, the kind that seemed to see past the surface.

She shook her head, trying to focus. Come on, Lila, she scolded herself. You barely know this guy. He could be married or living with three cats in a cramped studio. But despite her attempts to dismiss the moment, her heart wasn't easily convinced. She sighed, leaning back in her chair, her gaze drifting toward the framed photo of her family that sat on her desk. It reminded her of what her mother always said: "Good things come to those who wait, but great things come to those who make them happen."

It wasn't that she was waiting for her life to start. Lila was proud of what she had built—a promising career, loyal friends, and a studio apartment that felt like her sanctuary. But she couldn't deny that something felt missing, an undefined ache that the man in the bookstore had momentarily soothed.

When Friday finally arrived, her coworker and close friend, Sophie, cornered her at the office coffee machine.

"You've been distracted all week," Sophie said, handing Lila a steaming cup. "Spill it. What's going on?"

Lila hesitated, then gave a wry smile. "I met someone. Well, not met met. Just talked to him briefly in a bookstore. But he was... interesting."

Sophie raised an eyebrow, intrigued. "Interesting how? And more importantly, is he single and hot?"

Lila laughed, the tension easing. "I have no idea if he's single. But yes, he was... attractive. And smart. And..." She trailed off, her cheeks flushing.

"And?" Sophie prompted, grinning.

"And I don't know his name or how to find him again," Lila admitted, groaning.

"Well, that's tragic," Sophie said, patting her shoulder. "But don't overthink it. If it's meant to be, you'll see him again. You're a city girl now—strangers bump into each other all the time."

Lila smiled faintly, sipping her coffee. Sophie was right. Still, she couldn't help but wonder if fate would give her a second chance.

Ethan's Creative Frustrations

Across town, Ethan Hayes sat at his desk, staring at a blank canvas. The design pitch for his advertising agency was due in less than 48 hours, and he had nothing. His laptop screen showed the bare bones of a marketing campaign for a luxury shoe brand—a concept that felt as uninspired as it looked.

He ran a hand through his tousled hair and groaned. His usual spark, the ability to turn everyday objects into stories that sold themselves, seemed to have fizzled out.

"Creative block again?" his coworker Jonah asked, leaning against the edge of Ethan's desk.

Ethan sighed. "Something like that. This whole pitch feels hollow. I need a new angle, but it's just not coming together."

Jonah gave a sympathetic shrug. "Why don't you take a walk or something? Clear your head. That always helps you."

Ethan nodded absently. Jonah wasn't wrong. Whenever his creative well ran dry, he found inspiration in the rhythm of the city—the flicker of neon lights, the swirl of graffiti on old brick walls, the endless parade of people each living their own story. But today, even the thought of a walk didn't hold much appeal.

His thoughts drifted, unbidden, to the woman he'd met at the bookstore. He had replayed their conversation countless times over the past week, remembering the way she spoke with confidence about books and ideas, the way her smile had seemed to light up the entire store.

He sighed, leaning back in his chair. Bookstore girl. That's what he had started calling her in his head, and he hated how cliché it sounded. Still, there was something about her—a spark that made him feel alive in a way he hadn't in months.

"Alright," he muttered to himself, standing up and grabbing his coat. "A walk it is."

A Chance Meeting

The subway station was bustling with its usual symphony of city life. The metallic screech of trains echoed through the tunnels, accompanied by the rhythmic clatter of hurried footsteps and the occasional wail of a busker's violin. Lila descended the staircase, clutching her bag and weaving through the throng of commuters. She was heading to meet Sophie for dinner, and as usual, she was running late.

As she reached the platform, the familiar rumble of an approaching train vibrated through the air. She glanced around, her mind already preoccupied with deciding between Thai food or pizza.

That's when she saw him.

He was standing at the far end of the platform, leaning casually against a pillar. His profile was unmistakable—the sharp line of his jaw, the tousled dark hair that looked as though he had just run a hand through it.

Lila's breath hitched. It's him.

For a moment, she considered staying put, pretending she hadn't noticed. But something in her urged her forward.

Ethan, unaware of her approach, was lost in thought. He had stopped by the subway on a whim, hoping to take the train to the quieter outskirts of the city. His creative block still nagged at him, but the hum of the station had begun to stir ideas in his mind.

"Hi," came a voice from beside him.

He turned, startled, and there she was. Bookstore girl.

"Hey," he said, a smile spreading across his face. "It's you."

"Yeah," Lila said, returning the smile. "I thought I recognized you. From the bookstore."

Ethan nodded. "Small world, huh?"

Lila laughed softly. "Or maybe just a small city. What brings you here?"

He hesitated, then decided on honesty. "I was stuck on something for work and thought a change of scenery might help. And you?"

"Meeting a friend for dinner," she said. "Though now I feel like I've interrupted your moment of inspiration."

"Not at all," Ethan replied. "You're actually the best thing that's happened all week."

Lila blinked, caught off guard by his candidness. "Well, that's... unexpected. In a good way, I hope."

"Definitely in a good way," he said, holding her gaze.

The train screeched to a halt in front of them, the doors sliding open with a hiss. Neither of them moved to board, caught in the magnetic pull of their conversation.

"Do you—" they both began at the same time, then laughed.

"You first," Ethan said, gesturing for her to continue.

Lila hesitated. "Do you always go to that bookstore?"

"Not always," Ethan admitted. "But I might start. How about you?"

"Same," she said. "Maybe we'll run into each other again."

"Maybe," he said, though he hoped for something more certain.

The train doors chimed, warning of their imminent closure. Both of them stepped back instinctively, letting it leave without them.

"Ethan," he said suddenly, extending a hand.

"Lila," she replied, shaking it. His grip was firm but warm, and she felt a strange flutter in her chest.

The next train arrived moments later, and this time Lila stepped toward it. "This one's mine," she said, glancing back at him.

"Right," he said, feeling an inexplicable tug of disappointment. "Well, it was nice seeing you again, Lila."

"You too, Ethan," she said, smiling as the doors slid shut between them.

Growing Curiosity

As the train sped away, Lila found herself staring at her reflection in the glass. Her heart was racing, though she couldn't quite explain why.

Why didn't I ask for his number? she thought, already regretting it.

But the moment had passed, and she had to content herself with the thought that fate might throw them together once more.

For Ethan, the encounter left him both exhilarated and frustrated. He had finally learned her name—Lila—but she had disappeared again before he could make any plans.

He stood on the platform for a long moment, his thoughts swirling. Next time, he promised himself. Next time, I won't let her slip away.

Both of them left the station that evening with a growing sense of curiosity about the other. Their paths had crossed twice now, and something told them it wouldn't be the last time.

A Subtle Pull

The night seemed to linger longer than usual for both Lila and Ethan after their fleeting encounter at the subway station. Lila's dinner with Sophie was pleasant, yet her thoughts strayed repeatedly to Ethan. She replayed their brief conversation in her head, scrutinizing every detail—the way his eyes lit up when they spoke, the effortless humor in his words, and the inexplicable comfort she felt around him.

"I think I'll have the pad Thai," Sophie said, snapping Lila back to the present. "What about you?"

"Uh, same," Lila replied absently, her fork twirling a strand of her hair as she stared at the menu without really seeing it.

Sophie raised an eyebrow. "Okay, spill it. Who was on the subway platform? Because you're not even pretending to pay attention right now."

Lila sighed, a sheepish smile tugging at her lips. "It was him. The guy from the bookstore. Ethan."

Sophie's eyes widened. "What? That's like a rom-com waiting to happen! Did you talk to him? Did you exchange numbers? Tell me you didn't just let him walk away again."

Lila laughed at her friend's theatrics, though her cheeks burned with embarrassment. "We talked. Briefly. And no, we didn't exchange numbers. It just... didn't feel like the right moment."

Sophie groaned dramatically. "Lila! How many more 'moments' do you think the universe is going to hand you? You need to seize the day! Or at least the digits."

"I know, I know," Lila said, fiddling with the napkin in her lap. "But there was something nice about it. It wasn't rushed or awkward. It felt... natural. Like if we're meant to cross paths again, we will."

Sophie sighed, shaking her head. "You're such a romantic. Fine, I'll allow it. But if you see him again, promise me you'll do more than just exchange pleasantries."

"Promise," Lila said, though a part of her doubted she'd be so bold.

Ethan's Evening

Meanwhile, Ethan found himself nursing a cold beer at a small corner bar near his apartment. The dim lighting and low hum of conversation provided the perfect backdrop for his spiraling thoughts.

He couldn't shake the image of Lila from his mind—her laugh, the way her eyes crinkled at the corners when she smiled, the way her voice carried both warmth and intelligence. She had left an impression on him that was as surprising as it was enduring.

"Why the long face?" Jonah asked, sliding onto the stool beside him.

Ethan glanced up, startled. "Didn't know you'd be here."

"Thought you might need some company after your creative meltdown earlier," Jonah said, signaling the bartender for a drink. "But now it looks like there's something else on your mind. Care to share with the class?"

Ethan hesitated, then shrugged. "I ran into someone today. Someone I met last week at the bookstore."

"Bookstore girl?" Jonah asked, grinning.

Ethan groaned. "Don't call her that. Her name's Lila."

"Ah, progress," Jonah teased. "So, what's the deal? Did you ask her out? Exchange numbers? Or did you just awkwardly stare at each other until the train arrived?"

Ethan shot him a glare. "We talked. It was... nice. But no, I didn't get her number. She had to catch a train, and I didn't want to rush it."

Jonah rolled his eyes. "You've got to be kidding me. You're in one of the most densely populated cities in the world, and you think fate's just going to keep throwing her at you?"

Ethan frowned, taking a sip of his beer. "Maybe. I don't know. It felt... right to leave it where it was. Like if we're supposed to meet again, it'll happen."

Jonah smirked. "You've got it bad, man. But for your sake, I hope the universe is feeling generous."

The Intersection of What-Ifs

In the days that followed, both Lila and Ethan found themselves replaying their latest meeting, wondering what might have happened if they'd been braver, quicker, or just slightly less cautious. The city buzzed on around them, indifferent to their thoughts, yet each subway ride, each bookstore visit, carried a quiet hope.

Lila began to notice every dark-haired man in a crowd, her heart skipping for a moment before she realized it wasn't him. She made excuses to visit the bookstore again, lingering longer than usual in the hope of seeing him.

Ethan, too, felt the pull of possibility. He found himself detouring to that same subway station, scanning the faces of commuters with a vague sense of anticipation. He even stopped by the bookstore a few times, though he didn't linger long enough to make it obvious he was searching.

Each of them wondered: Was I foolish to leave it to chance?

A Shared Discovery

One evening, as the week was drawing to a close, Lila wandered into a small café near her office, her laptop in tow. She often worked there when she needed a change of scenery, and tonight, she had a manuscript to review that refused to hold her interest.

The café was warm and cozy, its walls lined with mismatched bookshelves and framed art. The smell of coffee and cinnamon lingered in the air, soothing her frayed nerves. She ordered a latte and settled into a corner table, opening her laptop and trying to focus.

At the same time, Ethan, weary from another day of grappling with creative block, decided to stop for coffee. He stepped into the café, immediately drawn to its welcoming atmosphere. As he scanned the room, his eyes landed on her.

For a moment, he hesitated, wondering if he was imagining things. But no—it was her. Lila, sitting at a corner table, her brow furrowed in concentration as she typed.

He took a deep breath and approached. "Hey," he said softly.

She looked up, startled, and then broke into a smile. "Ethan! What are you doing here?"

"I could ask you the same thing," he said, his grin mirroring hers.

"Just working," she said, gesturing to her laptop. "This place is my go-to when I need a break from the office."

"Looks like we have similar taste," he said, setting his coffee down on the edge of her table. "Mind if I join you?"

"Not at all," she said, closing her laptop.

They spent the next hour talking, their words flowing easily as they shared stories about their lives, their work, and their mutual love of books. The conversation felt effortless, as though they had known each other for years instead of mere weeks.

As the evening wore on, the question lingered in both their minds—Could this be something more?

Neither of them knew the answer, but for now, they were content to let the story unfold one chapter at a time.

Chapter 3: Digital Dating Woes

Lila's Adventures in the App World

"Okay, this is ridiculous," Sophie declared one Friday evening as she sat cross-legged on Lila's couch, scrolling through her phone. "You've got to put yourself out there, Lila. The bookstore guy—what's his name again? Ethan?—might've been cute, but you can't just wait around for fate to throw you together again."

Lila groaned, her face buried in a throw pillow. "Sophie, I'm not waiting. I just—ugh, I don't think dating apps are for me."

Sophie raised an eyebrow. "How would you know? Have you tried?"

"Well... no," Lila admitted, peeking out from behind the pillow.

"Exactly my point," Sophie said, grinning triumphantly. "You're going to set up a profile, and we're going to swipe until your finger cramps. Trust me, it'll be fun!"

Lila sighed but handed Sophie her phone. "Fine. But if this turns into a disaster, I'm holding you responsible."

Sophie beamed. "Deal. Now, let's get started."

An hour later, Lila's profile was live on Spark—a popular dating app Sophie swore by. Her bio read: Book lover, coffee enthusiast, and firm believer in the power of a good story. Looking for someone to make the plot twists of life a little sweeter. Sophie had insisted on adding a line about Lila's love for cats, even though Lila didn't own one, claiming it was "charmingly relatable."

The first few matches were promising—cute photos, witty bios—but as the chats began, things quickly went downhill.

The first guy, TravelTom87, seemed promising until he started every sentence with "As someone who's been to 17 countries..." and insisted on sharing unsolicited advice about how Lila could "broaden her horizons" by backpacking through Southeast Asia.

The second, PoetryKing_, quoted obscure sonnets in a way that felt more performative than genuine, ending every message with "Your move, milady."

The third, Chad420, didn't even make it past the first message: "u into crypto? let's collab."

By the end of the week, Lila was ready to delete the app. Sophie found the whole thing hilarious.

"You've got to admit, these stories are gold," Sophie said one evening as Lila recounted yet another awkward conversation over wine. "You could write a book about this."

"I'd rather not live it, thanks," Lila replied, rolling her eyes. "How is it so hard to find someone who's... normal?"

"Welcome to modern dating," Sophie said, raising her glass. "May the odds be ever in your favor."

Ethan's Set-Up Disaster

Meanwhile, Ethan was having his own share of romantic misadventures, courtesy of his well-meaning colleagues.

"Ethan, you're too much of a lone wolf," Jonah had said over lunch one day. "You need to get out there, meet people. I know someone perfect for you."

Ethan raised an eyebrow. "Define 'perfect.'"

"Relax," Jonah said, grinning. "Her name's Chloe. She's smart, funny, and she works in marketing. You two will hit it off."

Ethan reluctantly agreed, figuring one date couldn't hurt.

When the evening arrived, Chloe turned out to be, well, the opposite of what Ethan was looking for. She was lively and attractive, yes, but her version of "smart" involved quoting self-help books out of context, and her idea of "funny" was making loud jokes at the expense of their waiter.

"I just think people who don't have their lives together are dragging the rest of us down," Chloe said over appetizers, flipping her hair dramatically.

Ethan winced. "I think everyone's just doing their best," he said carefully.

Chloe waved her hand dismissively. "Oh, please. If you're not thriving, you're failing."

The conversation went downhill from there. By the time dessert arrived, Ethan was counting down the minutes until he could politely excuse himself.

When he finally escaped, Jonah called, eager for a post-mortem.

"So, how'd it go?" Jonah asked, barely able to contain his excitement.

Ethan sighed. "She's... not my type."

"Not your type how?"

"Not my type as in she thinks compassion is a weakness."

Jonah groaned. "Man, you're impossible to please."

"Or maybe you're just a terrible matchmaker," Ethan countered, hanging up before Jonah could respond.

Reflecting on the Digital Struggle

The following weekend, both Lila and Ethan found themselves pondering the state of modern romance, albeit in very different corners of the city.

Lila sat on her apartment balcony with a cup of tea, her phone resting on the table beside her. She had logged out of Spark, exhausted by the endless cycle of swiping, matching, and disappointment.

"What happened to meeting people the old-fashioned way?" she mused aloud to no one in particular.

She thought about her encounters with Ethan—the bookstore, the subway, his warm smile and easy conversation. It had felt effortless in a way that none of her app interactions had. Maybe Sophie was right; she needed to be bolder the next time their paths crossed. If there was a next time.

Across town, Ethan was sketching idly in his notebook at a small park near his apartment. His disastrous date with Chloe had only reinforced what he already knew: he wasn't interested in forced connections. He missed the serendipity of real moments—the way he had met Lila, for instance.

As his pencil moved across the page, he found himself sketching her face from memory. The details weren't perfect, but the expression—the curious tilt of her head, the glint of amusement in her eyes—was unmistakable.

He stared at the drawing for a long moment before closing the notebook with a sigh.

Serendipity Strikes

On a crisp Wednesday morning, the smell of freshly brewed coffee and pastries wafted through the air at Bloom Café, a charming spot nestled between two bookstores. Lila had decided to stop there before work, craving a quiet moment to herself before diving into another hectic day.

As she waited in line, she heard a familiar voice behind her.

"Lila?"

She turned, her heart skipping a beat. There he was—Ethan, looking slightly disheveled but undeniably handsome.

"Ethan! Hi," she said, unable to hide her surprise.

"Fancy seeing you here," he said, grinning. "Is this your usual spot?"

"Not really," she admitted. "Just needed a change of pace. You?"

"Same," he said, chuckling. "Though I think fate might have a hand in this one."

They both laughed, the initial awkwardness melting away.

After they got their coffee, they found a small table by the window and sat down, their conversation flowing as easily as it had the last time they met.

"So," Ethan said, leaning back in his chair, "any luck on the dating front?"

Lila groaned. "Don't get me started. Let's just say I've had my fair share of poetry kings and crypto bros."

Ethan laughed. "That bad, huh? I had a set-up recently that was... enlightening, to say the least."

"Enlightening how?" Lila asked, intrigued.

"Let's just say I learned the true meaning of the word 'thriving,'" he said with a smirk.

They shared their stories, laughing at the absurdities and commiserating over the challenges of finding genuine connections in a world that often felt too fast-paced and impersonal.

For the first time in weeks, both of them felt a sense of relief—a reminder that they weren't alone in their frustrations.

As their conversation stretched on, the morning sun streamed through the café window, casting a warm glow over their table. Neither of them noticed the time slipping by, nor did they particularly care.

Something unspoken passed between them—a quiet understanding that perhaps the connection they were both searching for had been right in front of them all along.

A Shift in the Conversation

As the warmth of their laughter ebbed, the conversation began to take on a quieter, more introspective tone. Lila stirred her latte absentmindedly, her eyes drifting toward the window. "It's funny," she said softly. "I spent so much time swiping through faces on an app, hoping for a spark. But with you..."

Ethan raised an eyebrow, leaning forward slightly. "With me?"

"It's just easy," she finished, her cheeks flushing slightly. "I don't have to overthink what to say, or worry about trying to sound interesting. It's just... natural."

Ethan's expression softened. "I feel the same way," he admitted. "The dating world these days—it feels like a constant performance. Like you're supposed to market yourself instead of just... be yourself. That's probably why I'm terrible at it."

Lila laughed lightly. "You? Terrible at dating? I find that hard to believe."

"Oh, it's true," Ethan said, his grin returning. "Just ask Jonah. He thinks I'm a lost cause. But maybe I'm just looking for the wrong things."

Lila tilted her head, intrigued. "And what are you looking for?"

He hesitated, his gaze steady on hers. "Something real. Someone I can talk to for hours without it feeling like work. Someone who makes me laugh, who makes me curious. Someone like..."

He trailed off, and Lila felt her heart skip a beat.

"Someone like the bookstore girl?" she teased, her voice soft.

Ethan chuckled, running a hand through his hair. "Exactly. Someone like the bookstore girl."

For a moment, silence settled between them, but it wasn't uncomfortable. It was the kind of silence that spoke volumes, charged with possibilities neither of them dared to voice yet.

Time Slips Away

When the café's lunch rush began, Lila glanced at her phone and let out a small gasp. "Oh no, I'm late for work!"

Ethan checked his watch and winced. "Me too. They're going to kill me if I'm late to another meeting."

They stood reluctantly, gathering their things. Lila hesitated as they reached the door, a sense of urgency bubbling up in her chest.

"Ethan," she said, turning to face him.

"Yeah?"

"Do you... maybe want to meet up again sometime? On purpose, I mean, not just by chance," she said, smiling nervously.

Ethan's face lit up. "I'd love that."

They exchanged numbers, and Lila couldn't help but laugh at the simplicity of it. After weeks of missed opportunities, it felt almost absurd how easy it was to make the connection official.

As they parted ways, Ethan couldn't stop smiling. The day's work awaited, but for the first time in weeks, he felt genuinely energized.

Lila, too, felt a buoyant lightness as she walked to her office. For all the digital frustrations and awkward first dates, the best connection she'd found had come from an old-fashioned meeting of chance.

Reflections and New Beginnings

That evening, Lila texted Sophie to share the news.

Lila: You'll never believe who I ran into today.

Sophie: The bookstore guy???

Lila: Yep. And this time, we exchanged numbers.

Sophie: FINALLY. Do I get credit for nudging the universe in your favor?

Lila: Sure, Sophie. You're basically Cupid.

Sophie's delighted response was almost as satisfying as the day's events. Almost.

Ethan, on the other hand, couldn't resist sending a text to Jonah.

Ethan: Remember how you said fate doesn't throw people together?

Jonah: Yeah?

Ethan: Turns out, it does.

Jonah's confusion was evident in his string of question marks, but Ethan didn't elaborate. He was too busy thinking about Lila—her laughter, her curiosity, the way she seemed to understand him without trying.

Both of them went to bed that night feeling the first hints of hope, the kind that comes from meeting someone who feels like a possibility.

The Next Step

Over the next few days, their texts became a steady rhythm—exchanging thoughts about books, sharing funny stories from their respective workplaces, and making tentative plans to meet up.

When the weekend arrived, Ethan suggested a trip to the bookstore where they had first met. Lila agreed instantly, charmed by the idea of returning to the place where it all began.

As they browsed the shelves together, their conversation flowed effortlessly, weaving between books and life and everything in between.

Lila picked up a novel she'd been meaning to read and held it up for Ethan's opinion.

"That one's great," he said. "But be warned—it'll break your heart."

"I can handle it," she said with a grin. "What about you? What's caught your eye?"

He held up a slim volume of poetry. "Something lighter. Balance, you know?"

Their laughter echoed softly through the aisles, and for the first time, they both felt the stirrings of something more.

This wasn't just serendipity anymore. It was the beginning of a story neither of them could wait to write.

Chapter 4: Building a Connection

Planning the Date

The week leading up to their first planned outing was charged with anticipation for both Lila and Ethan. Though their text exchanges had become frequent and effortless, there was a certain excitement—and nervousness—that came with the idea of meeting outside the safety net of messages and casual run-ins.

Ethan had suggested the date.

"There's this exhibit I've been meaning to check out," he had texted. "It's called Fractured Realities. A mix of surrealist art and interactive installations. Thought it might be fun."

Lila's curiosity had piqued immediately. "That sounds amazing. I'm in. Saturday?"

"Perfect. Be ready to have your mind blown."

As the day approached, Lila found herself obsessing over the details—what to wear, what to say, how to keep her lingering fears from bubbling to the surface.

"Relax," Sophie told her during one of their late-night calls. "You've already met him a few times. This isn't some high-stakes dinner with a stranger. Just be yourself."

"Easier said than done," Lila muttered, staring at her closet.

Ethan, meanwhile, was battling his own nerves. He wanted everything to be perfect, to prove that he wasn't like the other guys Lila might have dated.

"Don't overthink it, man," Jonah said when Ethan voiced his worries during their lunch break. "Just show up, make her laugh, and let the art do the rest."

"Easier said than done," Ethan replied, echoing Lila's words unknowingly.

A Quirky First Date

On Saturday, the day dawned crisp and clear, with a hint of fall in the air. Ethan arrived at the exhibit early, wanting to make sure everything went smoothly. The gallery was housed in a converted warehouse, its industrial exterior juxtaposed with the vibrant, modern art displayed through the glass windows.

When Lila arrived, Ethan's breath caught. She was dressed simply in a forest-green coat and black boots, her hair loose around her shoulders, but there was something about the way she carried herself that made her stand out.

"Hey," she said, smiling warmly as she approached.

"Hey," he replied, feeling his nerves melt away. "You look great."

"So do you," she said, taking in his casual-but-put-together look—a charcoal-gray sweater under a tailored jacket.

After a brief exchange of pleasantries, they stepped inside.

The exhibit was a sensory overload in the best way. The first room was filled with massive sculptures that seemed to defy gravity—blocks of stone suspended in midair, each reflecting shards of light that danced across the walls.

"This is incredible," Lila murmured, her eyes wide as she took it all in.

Ethan nodded, his gaze flicking between the art and her face. "Wait until you see the next room."

The second space was immersive, with a floor made of mirrored tiles and walls covered in moving projections of abstract images—swirling galaxies, cascading waterfalls, and shifting geometric patterns.

"Whoa," Lila breathed as they stepped inside. "It's like walking through a dream."

They wandered through the exhibit together, their conversation flowing as effortlessly as it always did.

"This one's my favorite," Ethan said, gesturing to a sculpture that looked like a fragmented human figure, its pieces held together by golden threads.

"Why?" Lila asked, tilting her head as she studied it.

"It reminds me of people," Ethan said after a moment. "We're all a little broken, but there's beauty in the way we hold ourselves together."

Lila glanced at him, surprised by the thoughtfulness of his answer. "That's... lovely," she said softly.

"What about you?" Ethan asked. "What's caught your eye?"

She pointed to a painting on the far wall—a vivid explosion of color that seemed to pulse with energy. "That one. It's chaotic but somehow balanced. Like life."

Ethan smiled. "I like that."

Shared Passions

As they moved through the gallery, their conversation drifted from art to literature, revealing the depth of their shared interests.

"Okay," Ethan said, stopping in front of a particularly surreal piece. "Desert island scenario: you can only bring three books. What do you choose?"

Lila laughed, tapping her chin in mock concentration. "Hmm. Pride and Prejudice, because I never get tired of Austen. The Great Gatsby, for the beauty of the writing. And... probably something practical, like a survival guide."

Ethan chuckled. "Smart. I was going to say Moby-Dick, but now I feel like I'd just starve to death while analyzing whale metaphors."

They both laughed, and Lila felt a warmth spreading through her chest.

"What about you?" she asked.

"1984, because it's terrifying but brilliant. The Catcher in the Rye, for nostalgia. And maybe a big, empty notebook so I could write my own story," Ethan said thoughtfully.

"That's a great answer," Lila said, smiling.

Their conversation continued as they left the gallery and wandered into the nearby park. The air was cool, and the golden afternoon light filtered through the trees, casting long shadows on the path.

They talked about their mutual love of travel—Lila's dream of visiting the lavender fields in Provence, Ethan's fascination with Japan's architecture.

"I think there's something magical about seeing the world through a different lens," Lila said, tucking a strand of hair behind her ear.

Ethan nodded. "It reminds you how small you are, in the best way."

Lila's Hesitation

As much as Lila enjoyed the date, a small part of her couldn't fully relax. It wasn't Ethan—he was kind, funny, and genuinely interested in her thoughts. But her past lingered in the back of her mind like an unwelcome guest.

Her last serious relationship had ended badly. Mark, her ex, had been charming at first but slowly revealed a manipulative side that left her questioning her worth. It had taken her a long time to rebuild her confidence, and the idea of letting someone in again—of risking that vulnerability—was daunting.

Ethan seemed different, but her instincts urged caution.

"Penny for your thoughts?" Ethan asked as they sat on a park bench, sipping coffee from a nearby vendor.

Lila hesitated, then smiled. "Just thinking about how much I've enjoyed today."

Ethan studied her for a moment, sensing there was more she wasn't saying. But he decided not to push.

"I've had a great time too," he said simply.

Ethan's Determination

Ethan, for his part, was determined to show Lila that she could trust him. He could sense her hesitation, though she tried to hide it behind her smiles.

As they walked back toward the subway station, he made a mental note to take things slow, to let her set the pace. He liked her too much to risk scaring her off.

When they reached the platform, they lingered near the edge, neither of them wanting the day to end.

"Thank you for today," Lila said, her voice warm but tinged with shyness.

"Thank you," Ethan said. "Let's do this again soon?"

"I'd like that," she said, her smile genuine.

As the train pulled in, they exchanged a quick hug—warm, but not too much—and parted ways.

On the ride home, Lila couldn't stop smiling. For the first time in a long while, she felt a spark of hope, fragile but unmistakable.

Ethan, too, felt a quiet satisfaction as he walked back to his apartment. The day had been better than he'd imagined, and he was already looking forward to the next chapter of their story.

This date was just the beginning. Both of them were aware that building a connection would take time, trust, and effort. But for now, they were content to let things unfold naturally, savoring the joy of discovering someone who felt like a kindred spirit.

The Morning After

The next morning, Lila woke to the soft glow of sunlight streaming through her bedroom window. For the first time in months, she felt a sense of lightness—a welcome reprieve from the usual weight of her thoughts. She lay in bed for a few minutes, replaying the highlights of the previous day.

Ethan's laugh. The way his eyes sparkled when he talked about his favorite books. His thoughtful response to the broken sculpture at the exhibit.

There had been something so effortless about being with him, and yet it wasn't without its complications. She could feel herself inching closer to letting her guard down, but the walls she had built after Mark were sturdy, forged in the fires of disappointment and heartbreak.

Sophie called around mid-morning, her voice buzzing with curiosity. "So? How was it? I need details. No, wait. I need all the details."

Lila laughed, pouring herself a cup of coffee. "It was great. We went to this amazing art exhibit, talked about books, and then wandered through the park. It was... easy, you know? Like we'd known each other forever."

Sophie let out a dramatic sigh. "That's so disgustingly cute. Tell me you're seeing him again soon."

"I think so," Lila said, smiling faintly. "But I'm trying not to overthink it. He's... different. In a good way. I just don't want to rush into anything and mess it up."

"You're not going to mess it up," Sophie assured her. "And honestly, after what you went through with Mark, you deserve someone who makes you feel good about yourself. Don't let fear hold you back, okay?"

Lila nodded, even though Sophie couldn't see her. "Okay. I'll try."

Ethan's Thoughts

Meanwhile, Ethan sat at his kitchen table, his sketchbook open in front of him. The page was filled with rough drawings of sculptures and abstract forms inspired by the art exhibit, but at the center of it all was a quick sketch of Lila, her hair swept back and her eyes alive with curiosity.

He hadn't intended to draw her. His pencil had moved almost of its own accord, as if his thoughts had needed a tangible outlet.

Jonah called shortly after, interrupting his reverie.

"Well?" Jonah said without preamble. "How'd it go?"

Ethan chuckled. "Good morning to you too."

"Don't stall. Did you charm her, or did you get in your own way?"

Ethan rolled his eyes. "It went well. Really well, actually. She's... amazing. Smart, funny, thoughtful. And I think she likes me, but..."

"But what?" Jonah prompted.

"There's something holding her back," Ethan admitted. "I can tell she's cautious, and I get it. I don't want to push her too fast."

Jonah was quiet for a moment. "You're a good guy, Ethan. If she's worth it—and it sounds like she is—then just keep showing up. That's half the battle."

Ethan smiled faintly. "Thanks, Jonah."

Planning the Next Step

Over the next few days, Ethan and Lila fell into an easy rhythm of texting, their conversations ranging from lighthearted banter to deeper topics. They talked about their favorite childhood memories, the places they'd traveled, and their hopes for the future.

"I don't know what I'd do without books," Lila texted one evening. "They've always been my escape when life gets tough."

"Same," Ethan replied. "Stories remind me that we're not alone. That someone, somewhere, has felt what we're feeling."

Their connection grew stronger with each exchange, but both of them knew that texting could only take them so far.

"You know," Ethan wrote one night, "I heard about this little jazz bar downtown. They have live music and a great vibe. Want to check it out this weekend?"

Lila hesitated for a moment before typing her reply.

"I'd love to."

A Quiet Moment

Saturday evening found them at a cozy jazz bar tucked away on a quiet side street. The space was dimly lit, with candles flickering on every table and a small stage where a quartet played soulful melodies.

Lila wore a simple black dress and a pair of understated earrings, her hair swept to one side. Ethan, in a navy blazer and crisp white shirt, looked effortlessly put together.

"This place is perfect," Lila said as they settled into their seats.

"I thought you'd like it," Ethan replied, his eyes warm.

As the music filled the room, their conversation flowed as easily as it had at the exhibit. They talked about everything and nothing, their words weaving together like the notes of the saxophone playing in the background.

At one point, Ethan reached across the table, his fingers brushing hers.

"Lila," he said softly, "I know we haven't known each other long, but I really like spending time with you. And I want you to know that I'm not in a rush. I'm okay with taking things slow, as long as it means getting to know you better."

Lila's heart swelled at his words. She met his gaze, her own vulnerability reflected in his eyes.

"I like spending time with you too," she said quietly. "And... I appreciate your patience. I just... I've been hurt before, and it's hard to trust again. But I'm trying."

"That's all I can ask for," Ethan said, his voice steady.

They sat in silence for a moment, the music washing over them like a gentle tide.

A Promise to Move Forward

As the evening wound down, Lila and Ethan stepped outside into the crisp night air. The city was alive with its usual hum, but for them, time seemed to slow.

"Can I walk you home?" Ethan asked.

Lila smiled. "I'd like that."

As they strolled through the quiet streets, their conversation turned to lighter topics—the quirks of city life, funny childhood memories, and the best pizza spots in town.

When they reached her building, Lila hesitated at the door.

"Thanks for tonight," she said, her voice soft.

"Anytime," Ethan replied, his smile reassuring.

Impulsively, Lila leaned in and kissed him on the cheek. It was brief, but the gesture spoke volumes.

"Goodnight, Ethan," she said, her cheeks flushed.

"Goodnight, Lila," he replied, watching as she disappeared inside.

As he walked home, Ethan felt a quiet sense of victory. He hadn't just had a great night—he'd taken another step toward building something real with Lila.

And Lila, lying in bed that night, felt a glimmer of hope she hadn't allowed herself to feel in years.

Their connection was still new, fragile, and filled with unanswered questions. But it was also filled with promise, and for now, that was enough.

Chapter 5: Conflicts and Missteps

A Major Opportunity for Lila

The email came on a gray Monday morning, cutting through the dull hum of the office like a lightning bolt. Lila's boss, Margot, had sent it with a cryptic subject line: Exciting Opportunity—Let's Discuss.

Sipping her coffee, Lila clicked the message open. The words practically leapt off the screen:

We've been chosen to pitch for the new Starling Publishing contract. It's huge. They want innovative voices, and I think you're the perfect person to lead the charge. Let's meet at 10 to go over the details.

Lila's heart raced. The Starling contract was the kind of career-defining opportunity she'd dreamed of—a chance to showcase her talent on a massive stage. Yet, the reality of it also hit hard: this would demand late nights, early mornings, and relentless focus for weeks, maybe even months.

By the time she stepped into Margot's office, Lila had resolved to give it her all.

"This is a game-changer for you, Lila," Margot said, handing her a thick packet of documents. "But it's going to take everything you've got."

"I'm ready," Lila said, her voice steady.

And she meant it. But as she left the meeting, her thoughts drifted to Ethan. How would this impact the fragile connection they'd been building?

Ethan's Unexpected Relocation

While Lila was diving headfirst into her new challenge, Ethan was blindsided by news of his own.

"Ethan, we've landed the Buchanan Motors campaign," his manager announced during their weekly meeting. "They've requested you personally to oversee the creative direction. You'll need to be in Chicago for the next three months."

"Chicago?" Ethan echoed, startled.

"I know it's short notice," his manager said, "but this is a big deal. The campaign could catapult your career."

Ethan nodded slowly, trying to process the news. The Buchanan Motors account was one of the most prestigious projects his firm had ever secured. Yet, the timing couldn't have been worse.

His mind immediately went to Lila. Things between them were still new and delicate, and the thought of leaving just as they were finding their footing filled him with unease.

That evening, he called Jonah.

"Three months isn't that long," Jonah said, trying to sound reassuring. "And Chicago's not Mars. You can still keep things going with Lila."

"Yeah, but what if she takes it the wrong way? Like I'm bailing on us before we even start?" Ethan asked.

"You're overthinking this," Jonah said. "Just be honest with her. If she's worth it, she'll understand."

Ethan hoped Jonah was right.

Miscommunications Begin

The next few weeks were a whirlwind for both Lila and Ethan. Lila spent long hours at the office, poring over manuscripts and perfecting her pitch for Starling Publishing. Late nights became the norm, and her phone often sat neglected on her desk.

Ethan, meanwhile, was preparing for his relocation. Between packing, planning, and finalizing campaign details, he barely had time to breathe. He texted Lila whenever he could, but their exchanges grew shorter and less frequent.

One evening, as Lila sat at her desk in the dim glow of her apartment, her phone buzzed.

Ethan: Hey, haven't heard from you today. Everything okay?

She stared at the screen for a moment before typing back:

Lila: Just busy with work. You?

His reply came quickly.

Ethan: Same. Chicago prep is kicking my ass.

She frowned. She knew Ethan had mentioned the project, but she hadn't realized it involved leaving the city.

Lila: Wait, you're going to Chicago?

Ethan: Yeah, for a campaign. Three months. I thought I told you.

Lila felt a pang of annoyance. He "thought" he told me?

Lila: You didn't. When do you leave?

Ethan: Friday.

Her stomach sank. That was only three days away.

Lila: That's soon.

Ethan: Yeah. Timing sucks.

Lila stared at the screen, frustration bubbling beneath the surface. She wanted to tell him how blindsided she felt, how unfair it seemed for him to drop this on her at the last minute. But before she could type another word, her laptop chimed with an incoming email.

"Work," she muttered, pushing her phone aside.

Ethan stared at his phone, waiting for a response that didn't come.

The Breaking Point

By Friday evening, the tension between them was palpable. Ethan had asked Lila to meet him for coffee before he left, but she showed up late, visibly frazzled.

"Sorry," she said, sliding into the seat across from him. "The pitch is next week, and Margot's been breathing down my neck."

"It's fine," Ethan said, though his tone was clipped.

They sat in awkward silence for a moment before Lila spoke.

"So, Chicago," she said, trying to sound casual. "Are you excited?"

"Not really," Ethan admitted. "I hate the timing, but it's a big deal for my career."

Lila nodded, but her expression was unreadable. "It just feels like you've been pulling away lately."

"Pulling away?" Ethan repeated, incredulous. "Lila, I've been trying to stay connected, but you're the one who's been too busy to respond half the time."

Lila bristled. "I'm working on something huge, Ethan. It's not like I'm ignoring you on purpose."

"And you think I am?" Ethan shot back. "I'm doing the best I can, but it feels like you're more focused on your job than on us."

"Us?" Lila said, her voice rising. "Are we even an 'us'? Because right now, it feels like two people pretending to make time for each other."

Ethan flinched, the words cutting deeper than he expected. "You think I don't care about this? About you?"

"I don't know, Ethan," Lila said, her voice cracking. "You're leaving, and you didn't even bother to talk to me about it. What does that say?"

Ethan exhaled sharply, running a hand through his hair. "You're right. I should've told you sooner. But I didn't because I didn't want to add to your stress. And honestly, Lila, I didn't know where we stood."

Lila stared at him, her emotions warring between anger and hurt. "I just... I don't know if I can do this right now," she said softly.

Ethan's jaw tightened, but he nodded. "Maybe you're right. Maybe the timing's all wrong."

They sat in heavy silence, the weight of their words settling over them.

Uncertain Futures

When they parted ways that night, both Lila and Ethan felt a hollow ache in their chests.

Ethan boarded his flight to Chicago the next morning, replaying their argument in his head. Had he pushed too hard? Should he have tried harder to reassure her?

Lila, meanwhile, threw herself into her work, using the Starling pitch as a distraction. Yet, no matter how busy she stayed, thoughts of Ethan crept in—his smile, his laugh, the way he had seemed to truly see her.

They had come so far in such a short time, and now it felt like everything was unraveling.

But neither of them was ready to give up entirely. Deep down, they both hoped that this was just a chapter of conflict—not the end of their story.

Reflection and Regret

The days following their argument were heavy with regret for both Lila and Ethan. The distance between them, both physical and emotional, felt unbearable yet insurmountable.

For Ethan, life in Chicago was a whirlwind. The Buchanan Motors campaign demanded his full attention, with endless meetings, brainstorming sessions, and late nights at the agency's downtown office. Yet, even amidst the chaos, his thoughts constantly drifted back to Lila.

He replayed their last conversation over and over, dissecting every word, every pause. He hated how things had ended, how he'd left without fixing what had gone wrong.

One evening, after a particularly grueling day, Ethan found himself scrolling through his photos. There weren't many of Lila—just a few candid shots from their bookstore outing and the art exhibit. But even those small glimpses were enough to bring a pang of longing.

Jonah called to check in that night, sensing his friend's mood from miles away.

"You're overthinking it, man," Jonah said. "These things happen. She's probably just stressed with work. Give her some space, and then reach out. Clear the air."

Ethan nodded, though doubt still gnawed at him. What if she didn't want to talk?

Lila, meanwhile, was in a similar state of turmoil. The Starling pitch was days away, and she had poured every ounce of energy into perfecting it. Yet, no matter how busy she was, thoughts of Ethan lingered at the edges of her mind.

She missed him. Missed the way he made her laugh, the way he listened so intently when she spoke. But she also felt a simmering resentment—toward him for leaving without really discussing it, and toward herself for not handling the situation better.

One evening, as she sat alone in her apartment, staring at the draft of her pitch, Sophie called.

"Okay, spill it," Sophie demanded. "You've been weird all week. What's going on with you and Ethan?"

Lila hesitated, then sighed. "We fought. Before he left for Chicago."

Sophie's tone softened. "What happened?"

"It just... felt like we were on different pages," Lila admitted. "He thought I wasn't making enough time for him, and I thought he was pulling away. Everything just blew up."

"Do you still like him?" Sophie asked gently.

"Of course I do," Lila said, her voice breaking slightly. "But I don't know if it's enough. He's there, I'm here, and I don't know how to make it work."

"Lila," Sophie said firmly, "if you care about him, don't let this slip away. Talk to him. Figure it out together. Relationships aren't supposed to be perfect—they're supposed to be worth it."

Attempts at Communication

A week later, after the Starling pitch had been delivered and Ethan had settled into his new routine, both of them found themselves reaching for their phones.

Lila typed and deleted a dozen drafts of a message before finally settling on something simple:

Lila: Hey. Hope Chicago's treating you well.

Ethan saw the message pop up just as he was leaving a late meeting. His heart leapt, but he took a deep breath before replying.

Ethan: Hey. It's been a lot of work, but I'm surviving. How are you?

The exchange was cautious, like two people testing the waters, but it was a start. Over the next few days, they texted sporadically, avoiding the deeper topics they knew they needed to discuss.

One night, Ethan decided to take the plunge.

Ethan: I miss talking to you. Really talking. Can we call sometime?

Lila stared at the message, her chest tightening. She missed him too, but the idea of a real conversation made her nervous.

Lila: I miss it too. How about tomorrow night?

A Difficult Conversation

The next evening, Lila sat curled up on her couch, her phone in hand. She had rehearsed what she wanted to say a dozen times, but when Ethan's name lit up her screen, her mind went blank.

"Hi," she said softly.

"Hi," Ethan replied. There was a pause, but it wasn't as awkward as she'd feared.

"How's Chicago?" she asked.

"Busy," Ethan said. "But good. The project's coming together. What about you? How'd the pitch go?"

"We got the contract," Lila said, a small smile creeping into her voice.

"That's amazing," Ethan said, his tone warm. "I'm so proud of you."

"Thanks," she said, her smile fading slightly. "Ethan, I... I'm sorry about before. About how I handled everything."

He exhaled softly. "I'm sorry too. I should've told you about Chicago sooner. I just didn't know how to balance everything."

"Neither did I," Lila admitted. "I think I was scared. Scared of getting too close, of letting someone in again."

Ethan was quiet for a moment. "I get it. I've been scared too. But Lila... I want this to work. I don't know how yet, but I want to try."

Tears pricked at Lila's eyes. "I want to try too. But long-distance... it's not easy."

"No, it's not," Ethan agreed. "But we can figure it out. One step at a time."

For the first time in weeks, Lila felt a glimmer of hope.

A Fragile Truce

In the days that followed, they made a concerted effort to stay connected. Their schedules were still demanding, but they found time for video calls and messages, sharing the little details of their lives that kept them grounded.

It wasn't perfect, and there were still moments of doubt and frustration. But both Lila and Ethan knew that the best stories were rarely without conflict.

And they weren't ready to close the book on theirs just yet

Chapter 6: The Distance Between Us

Lila's Inner Struggle

Lila sat on the floor of her apartment, a glass of red wine in one hand and a photo album in the other. She had been cleaning earlier, but as usual, the task had morphed into a trip down memory lane.

The photo album was from her college years, filled with snapshots of friendships that had grown and faded, vacations with family, and, toward the back, pictures of her ex, Mark.

She frowned as she flipped through the pages, her chest tightening when she saw their smiling faces. At the time, she'd thought they had something unshakable. He had been charming and attentive, but over time, his criticisms had chipped away at her self-esteem. His words, though subtle, had planted seeds of doubt that took years to uproot.

Now, with Ethan, those old fears were creeping back in. She didn't doubt his intentions—he had been nothing but kind and supportive. But she questioned herself.

Am I capable of being in a relationship without losing myself?

She closed the album with a sigh and leaned back against the couch, staring at the ceiling. She wanted to be with Ethan, but she also valued the independence she'd fought so hard to reclaim. Balancing the two felt like an impossible equation.

Her phone buzzed beside her. It was Sophie, FaceTiming as she often did unannounced. Lila debated letting it ring but decided against it, swiping to answer.

"Hey," she said, forcing a smile.

"Wow, that's convincing," Sophie said, raising an eyebrow. "What's going on? You look like someone stole your last piece of chocolate."

Lila chuckled despite herself. "I'm just... thinking."

"Dangerous territory," Sophie teased, then softened her tone. "What about?"

"Ethan," Lila admitted. "And me. And whether I can actually make this work without losing myself in the process."

Sophie sighed, resting her chin on her hand. "Lila, I get it. After everything with Mark, it makes sense to feel this way. But Ethan isn't Mark. He's shown you time and again that he respects you and your independence. You just have to let him in a little more."

"I'm trying," Lila said quietly.

"Good," Sophie said, smiling. "Because you deserve someone who makes you happy. And from the way you light up when you talk about him, I know Ethan does."

Lila felt a small flicker of hope ignite in her chest. Maybe Sophie was right.

Ethan's Life in His New City

Ethan sat in his temporary apartment in Chicago, a beer in hand and the city skyline glittering beyond the windows. The Buchanan Motors campaign was going well—better than he'd expected—but success felt hollow without Lila to share it with.

He had tried to stay busy, exploring the city when he wasn't working. Chicago had its charms: the food, the art, the architecture. But every time he stumbled upon something he thought Lila would like, the ache of missing her grew stronger.

He picked up his phone, scrolling through their recent texts. Their conversations had been light lately, focused on the surface-level details of their lives. It felt safer that way, but it wasn't enough.

Jonah called, breaking Ethan's reverie.

"What's up, Chicago hotshot?" Jonah said, his voice teasing.

"Not much," Ethan replied, leaning back against the couch.

Jonah paused, his tone turning serious. "Okay, cut the act. How are things with Lila?"

Ethan sighed. "Complicated. We're talking, but it feels... distant. Like neither of us knows how to bridge the gap."

Jonah was quiet for a moment before speaking. "Look, man, you've got to decide what you want. If Lila's the one, you can't let fear or distance get in the way. You've got to fight for it. Relationships aren't easy, but the good ones are worth the work."

Ethan nodded, Jonah's words sinking in. Maybe it was time to stop playing it safe.

The Impact of Separation

As the weeks passed, the distance between them began to take its toll.

For Lila, the silence between their messages felt like an unspoken accusation. She worried that Ethan was losing interest, that the distance had become too much for him.

For Ethan, the growing gap between them felt like failure. He worried that Lila's independence meant she didn't need him as much as he needed her.

Both of them found themselves reflecting on their past relationships and what they truly wanted from love.

Lila thought about how she had always been the one to compromise, to bend herself into the shape of what her partner needed. She didn't want that anymore. She wanted a love where both people could grow together without losing themselves.

Ethan thought about how he had always been the one to hold back, to protect himself from getting hurt. He didn't want that anymore. He wanted a love where he could be vulnerable, where he could show someone his whole self without fear.

Heartfelt Advice

One afternoon, Lila visited her parents for lunch. Her mother, a pragmatic but kind woman, noticed her daughter's distraction immediately.

"Okay, spill," her mom said as she set a plate of sandwiches on the table. "What's going on?"

"It's Ethan," Lila admitted. "We've been... distant. And I don't know how to fix it."

Her mom sat down across from her, studying her with a thoughtful expression.

"Do you care about him?" her mom asked.

"Of course," Lila said.

"Then stop overthinking and talk to him," her mom said simply. "Real connections don't happen every day, Lila. Don't let fear get in the way of something that could be wonderful."

Meanwhile, in Chicago, Ethan was having a similar conversation with his sister, Claire, who had driven in from a nearby suburb to visit.

"Let me get this straight," Claire said, setting down her coffee. "You're crazy about this girl, but you're afraid to tell her because she might not feel the same way?"

Ethan nodded, feeling sheepish.

"Ethan," Claire said, her tone gentle but firm, "love isn't about guarantees. It's about taking the leap. If you care about her, you owe it to yourself—and to her—to try."

A New Resolve

That evening, both Lila and Ethan sat down with their phones, hearts pounding as they drafted their messages.

Lila: I've been thinking about us a lot lately. Can we talk?

Ethan: I miss you. Can we have a real conversation?

When their messages crossed paths, both of them smiled, feeling a glimmer of hope for the first time in weeks.

The conversation that followed was honest and raw, filled with apologies, reassurances, and promises to try harder.

By the end of the call, the distance between them didn't feel so insurmountable. It felt like something they could overcome together.

And for the first time in a long while, they both felt at peace.

Chapter 7: Small Steps Toward Reconciliation

The days following the turmoil between Lila and Ethan were quiet but heavy, filled with unspoken thoughts and questions about whether the rift between them could ever be bridged. Despite the hurt that lingered on both sides, a faint thread of connection remained, pulling them back toward each other. Neither wanted to admit it openly, but they missed the other—the inside jokes, the way they understood each other's quirks, and the comfort of shared memories.

It was Lila who took the first step.

Lila's Care Package

Lila sat cross-legged on the floor of her small apartment, surrounded by a mix of tissue paper, cardboard boxes, and a carefully chosen assortment of items. She wasn't the type to make grand gestures, but as she sifted through her collection, she wanted this to feel personal—a reflection of the bond she still felt with Ethan, even after everything.

At the heart of the care package was a book: "The Stars We Watch," an anthology of short stories about space exploration and human connection. The book wasn't just any book—it was the one Lila had been reading on the day she and Ethan first met, years ago, in a bustling coffee shop downtown. Ethan had noticed her struggling to balance her coffee, her laptop, and the book all at once, and had offered a charmingly awkward hand.

She smiled faintly at the memory.

"I thought of you when I reread this," she murmured, holding the book in her hands as if it contained a part of their history.

She tucked it into the box along with a bag of his favorite coffee beans, a small sketch she'd drawn of a nebula (a nod to Ethan's fascination with astronomy), and a handwritten note:

"Ethan,

I've been thinking a lot about us lately. I don't know if this can fix anything, but I wanted to share something that reminded me of when we first met—when everything felt simple. I hope this brings a smile to your face, even for a moment.

Take care,

Lila"

Her hand hesitated for a moment before she placed the note on top and sealed the box. It was a small step, a way to reach out without demanding too much.

Ethan Receives the Package

Two days later, Ethan arrived home to find the care package waiting for him. He frowned, puzzled, as he picked it up from the doorstep. The handwriting on the label was unmistakably Lila's, and his heart skipped a beat.

He carried the box to his kitchen table, setting it down carefully as if it were fragile. For a moment, he just stared at it, debating whether to open it. They hadn't spoken since their last argument, and the sudden arrival of the package caught him off guard.

Finally, curiosity won.

Inside, he found the book, the coffee, the sketch, and the note. The sight of the book stopped him in his tracks. His mind flashed back to that first day in the coffee shop, to Lila's laughter when she spilled a bit of coffee on her own book and tried to laugh it off as if she wasn't embarrassed.

He picked up the note, reading it slowly, then rereading it. Her words felt raw and sincere, cutting through the tension that had built between them.

Ethan ran a hand through his hair, the weight of his emotions catching him off guard. He hadn't realized how much he missed her until this moment.

Ethan's Decision to Visit

Later that evening, Ethan sat on the edge of his couch, staring at the book on his coffee table. The note was folded neatly beside it. His apartment felt emptier than usual, the silence pressing in on him.

He had tried to give Lila space, convincing himself that it was what she wanted. But the care package felt like an olive branch, a subtle invitation to reconnect.

For the first time in weeks, he allowed himself to think about what he wanted. He thought about Lila's laugh, the way she'd light up when she was passionate about something, and the way she always seemed to understand him even when he didn't say much.

It wasn't enough to sit and wait anymore. He had to do something.

The decision came suddenly, almost impulsively: he was going to see her.

The Visit

The next morning, Ethan stood nervously outside Lila's apartment building, a bouquet of pale yellow daisies in his hand. He remembered her saying once that yellow flowers made her smile because they reminded her of sunshine on cloudy days.

He hesitated, questioning whether this was the right move. What if she wasn't ready to see him? What if she didn't want him here at all?

Summoning his courage, he knocked on her door.

A few seconds passed, and then the door opened. Lila stood there in her favorite oversized sweater, her hair tied loosely back. Her eyes widened in surprise when she saw him.

"Ethan," she said, her voice soft.

"Hey," he replied, shifting awkwardly on his feet. He held out the daisies. "I, uh, thought you might like these."

She blinked, then smiled faintly, taking the flowers from him. "Thank you. They're beautiful."

"Can I come in?" he asked hesitantly.

After a moment, she stepped aside.

An Honest Conversation

They sat across from each other at her small kitchen table, a mug of tea in Lila's hands and a cup of coffee in Ethan's. For a moment, neither of them spoke. The tension was palpable, but there was also a sense of relief in finally being face-to-face.

"I got your package," Ethan began. "Thank you. It meant... a lot."

Lila nodded, her fingers tracing the rim of her mug. "I wasn't sure if I should send it. I didn't know if you'd want to hear from me."

"I did," Ethan said quickly. "I do. I just... I didn't know how to reach out. I didn't want to make things worse."

Lila met his gaze, her expression vulnerable. "I think we both made mistakes. I've been thinking a lot about what went wrong, and I know I wasn't as open with you as I should have been. I kept things bottled up, and it wasn't fair to you."

"And I should've listened more," Ethan admitted. "I got defensive when I should've been trying to understand you. I let my own fears get in the way."

They sat in silence for a moment, letting the weight of their words settle.

Agreeing to Take Things Slow

"I don't know if we can fix everything," Lila said quietly, "but I'd like to try. If you're willing."

Ethan nodded, his expression earnest. "I want to try too. But maybe this time, we focus on the small things. One step at a time."

Lila smiled softly. "That sounds like a good idea. No rushing, no pressure. Just... honest communication."

Ethan reached across the table, his hand hovering for a moment before she took it. "Thank you," he said. "For giving me another chance."

"It's not about chances," Lila replied. "It's about understanding each other better. And I think we're finally starting to do that."

A Small Step Forward

They spent the rest of the afternoon talking—not about their past arguments or their mistakes, but about the things they loved and missed. They laughed over shared memories, from the time Ethan burned dinner so badly that they had to order pizza, to the late-night road trip where they ended up stranded at a gas station for hours.

For the first time in weeks, the air between them felt lighter.

As Ethan left Lila's apartment that evening, the care package in his arms and a tentative smile on his face, he felt a flicker of hope. They weren't back to where they used to be, but they were on their way.

And for now, that was enough.

Reflecting on the Visit

That evening, after Ethan left, Lila sat alone at her kitchen table, the faint scent of daisies wafting from the vase where she had arranged the flowers. Her fingers absentmindedly traced the rim of her tea mug as she replayed the day's events in her mind.

She hadn't expected to see him, not like this. The look on his face when he handed her the flowers had been raw—unguarded in a way Ethan rarely allowed himself to be. That vulnerability reminded her of why she had fallen for him in the first place.

Lila reached for her journal, something she had been using more often in the weeks they'd been apart. It had become a way to process her thoughts without the weight of expectation or judgment. Flipping to a blank page, she began to write:

"Today, Ethan showed up at my door with daisies and an apology. It's strange how something so simple can feel so monumental. We talked, really talked, for the first time in a long while. There's still so much to say, but for the first time, I feel like we're moving forward—together."

She closed the journal, letting out a deep breath. It wasn't perfect, and it wouldn't be for a while, but it was a start.

Ethan's Reflection

Meanwhile, Ethan sat on his couch, the care package Lila had sent sitting on the coffee table in front of him. He had already skimmed through the book, rereading some of the passages that had once sparked their first conversation years ago. The scent of the coffee beans she'd included filled the room, grounding him in the present even as his thoughts lingered on the past.

Lila's sketch of the nebula lay beside him. Her drawings had always amazed him—not just because of her skill but because of the way she seemed to capture something unspoken in her work. This one, with its swirling colors and stark contrasts, felt like it mirrored their relationship: chaotic yet beautiful.

For the first time in weeks, Ethan felt like the walls he had built around himself were starting to crumble. Lila's care package hadn't just been a gesture—it had been an invitation. And today, when he'd stood at her door, it was as though she had accepted his presence in her life once again.

The Days That Follow

True to their promise, Ethan and Lila didn't rush. They eased into a rhythm of communication, exchanging texts and phone calls that were lighthearted but meaningful.

One morning, Ethan sent Lila a picture of the nebula sketch, now framed and hanging on the wall above his desk.

"Found the perfect spot for this. I see it every time I sit down to work. Thank you."

Her reply came quickly.

"I'm glad you like it. That one's always been one of my favorites."

Later that week, Lila sent Ethan a text with a picture of her daisies blooming in their vase.

"Still going strong. You chose well. :)"

These small exchanges felt like a lifeline, pulling them closer without the weight of expectation.

A Walk in the Park

Two weeks later, Ethan suggested meeting in person again. "No pressure," he said over the phone. "I was thinking something simple, like a walk in the park. We don't even have to talk about us—just... spend some time together."

Lila hesitated for a moment before agreeing. "Okay. I'd like that."

They met on a sunny Saturday afternoon, the crisp autumn air carrying the faint scent of fallen leaves. The park was alive with activity—children playing, joggers passing by, couples walking hand-in-hand. Ethan arrived first, standing awkwardly near a bench until he saw Lila approaching, her scarf fluttering in the breeze.

"Hey," she said, smiling softly.

"Hey," Ethan replied, falling into step beside her as they started down the path.

The conversation was easy, focusing on everyday topics: a new café Lila had tried, a podcast Ethan had been listening to, the strange weather that had settled over the city. But there were moments of quiet, too—comfortable silences where they simply walked, enjoying each other's company without the need to fill the gaps.

As they rounded a bend, they came across a small pond. The water was still, reflecting the golden hues of the surrounding trees. Lila stopped, gazing at the scene.

"Do you remember that time we went canoeing and almost tipped over?" she asked, a playful smile tugging at her lips.

Ethan laughed. "I remember you laughing so hard you couldn't paddle, and I had to do all the work."

"You were so grumpy," she teased, nudging him lightly with her elbow.

"I wasn't grumpy," he protested. "I was... focused."

"Focused on not falling in," Lila said, grinning.

They both laughed, the sound carrying across the water.

A Moment of Vulnerability

As they continued walking, Ethan grew quiet. Lila noticed the change in his demeanor and turned to him. "What's on your mind?"

He hesitated, his hands shoved into his pockets. "I've been thinking a lot about why things went wrong between us," he said finally. "I keep replaying our arguments, wondering what I could've done differently."

Lila stopped, placing a hand on his arm. "Ethan, we both made mistakes. This isn't about placing blame—it's about learning from it and doing better."

He looked at her, his eyes filled with a mixture of regret and hope. "I just don't want to mess this up again. You mean too much to me."

Her expression softened. "Ethan, we're both scared. But the fact that we're here, trying—that means something. We're not perfect, and we never will be. But we're still here."

He nodded, a small smile tugging at the corners of his mouth. "Thanks, Lila."

A Step Toward Healing

By the time they left the park, the sun was beginning to set, casting the sky in shades of pink and orange. Ethan walked Lila to her car, the easy rhythm of their earlier conversation lingering between them.

"I had a good time today," Lila said, leaning against the driver's side door.

"Me too," Ethan replied. "Maybe we could do this again sometime?"

She smiled. "I'd like that."

As she drove away, Ethan stood in the parking lot for a moment, watching her taillights disappear around the corner. For the first time in a long time, he felt like they were heading in the right direction.

Hope for the Future

That evening, Lila texted Ethan:

"Thanks for today. It felt like a fresh start."

His reply came almost instantly.

"It was. Let's keep taking those small steps."

And for the first time, both of them allowed themselves to believe that reconciliation wasn't just possible—it was within reach.

Chapter 8: The Grand Gesture

The weeks passed in a blur for Ethan. His project—a complex architectural design for a public library in a small coastal town—had consumed his time and energy for months. But even in the midst of deadlines, his thoughts often drifted to Lila.

Every call, every text, and every memory of their recent conversations reinforced his determination to prove to her—and to himself—that they could build something lasting.

Ethan knew he didn't just want reconciliation; he wanted a fresh start. And that would require more than words—it would require action, a gesture that would show Lila how deeply he cared.

Finishing the Project

Ethan worked tirelessly to complete his project, pouring his heart into every detail. The library design was inspired by everything he had learned about Lila—her love for books, her appreciation for cozy, quiet spaces, and her passion for creating connections between people and stories.

The centerpiece of the design was a large reading room with floor-to-ceiling windows, allowing natural light to pour in. Ethan imagined Lila there, sitting by a window with a book in her hands, and it fueled his drive to finish.

Finally, after countless late nights and revisions, the project was complete. As he sent off the final designs to his client, a sense of accomplishment washed over him—but it was quickly followed by nervous anticipation.

He had made up his mind. It was time to return to New York and surprise Lila.

The Bookstore Surprise

The bookstore where they had first met was a quaint, independent shop nestled on a quiet corner of Manhattan. Its creaky wooden floors and towering shelves gave it an almost magical quality, a place where time seemed to slow down.

Lila often came here to browse, finding comfort in the familiar scent of old paper and ink. She didn't expect to see Ethan again so soon, certainly not here, in this place that held so much history for them.

Ethan stepped inside, the sound of the bell above the door making Lila glance up from the display table she was rearranging. Her breath caught when she saw him standing there, dressed in a navy coat and holding a small, wrapped package in his hands.

"Ethan?" she said, her voice a mix of surprise and disbelief.

"Hi, Lila," he said, his lips curving into a tentative smile. "I finished my project early and thought I'd stop by."

Lila set down the stack of books she was holding, her hands trembling slightly. "You're... here?"

"I'm here," Ethan said, stepping closer. "And I was hoping you might let me buy you a coffee. Or tea. Or whatever it is you drink these days."

A smile broke across her face, soft but genuine. "I think I can spare some time for an old friend."

The Heartfelt Conversation

They found a small table in the back corner of the bookstore's café, a cozy spot surrounded by shelves lined with vintage books. The conversation started light—catching up on Ethan's project, Lila's work at the bookstore, and the random quirks of city life.

But as the minutes passed, the conversation turned deeper.

"I've been thinking a lot about us," Ethan said, his voice steady but quiet. "About what went wrong and what I could've done differently."

Lila stirred her tea, her gaze thoughtful. "You weren't the only one who made mistakes, Ethan. I kept so much bottled up because I was afraid of being vulnerable. I thought it was easier to just... hold it all in."

"And I didn't make it easy for you to open up," Ethan admitted. "I put up walls too. Maybe we were both scared of the same thing—letting someone see the messy parts of us."

Lila smiled faintly. "The messy parts are where the real connection happens, though, aren't they?"

Ethan nodded, reaching across the table to take her hand. "Lila, I want us to try again. But I don't just want to pick up where we left off—I want us to build something new. Something better."

Her eyes softened as she looked at him, her hand resting comfortably in his. "I want that too, Ethan. But I think we need to keep taking it slow—one step at a time."

He smiled. "Slow is fine. As long as we're moving forward together."

The Grand Gesture

Later that evening, Ethan accompanied Lila back to her apartment. They climbed the stairs together, their conversation punctuated by comfortable silences. As they reached her door, Ethan hesitated, a hint of nervousness flickering across his face.

"What is it?" Lila asked, tilting her head.

"There's something I've been working on," he said, holding up the small, wrapped package he'd brought with him. "It's... a little something for you. I wanted to show you how much you mean to me."

Lila's brow furrowed in curiosity as she accepted the package and carefully unwrapped it. Inside was a beautifully hand-drawn sketch of a cozy reading nook—complete with a built-in bookshelf, a plush chair, and a window seat with soft cushions.

"This is... my apartment," Lila said, her voice filled with surprise. "You sketched this for me?"

"I did," Ethan said, rubbing the back of his neck sheepishly. "I remembered how you always talked about wanting a little corner to read and unwind. So I thought... why not make it happen?"

Lila looked up at him, her eyes shining. "You want to build this for me?"

Ethan nodded. "If you'll let me."

Building the Nook

The next few days were filled with a mix of excitement and chaos as Ethan and Lila worked together to transform a small, underutilized corner of her apartment into the reading nook of her dreams.

Ethan brought over tools and supplies, meticulously measuring and cutting wood for the shelves and window seat. Lila helped where she could, holding boards steady and offering suggestions for the design.

As they worked, they fell into an easy rhythm, their conversations lighthearted and filled with laughter.

"You know," Lila said one afternoon, brushing sawdust off her hands, "I never thought you'd be the type to take on a DIY project."

Ethan grinned. "You'd be surprised what I'm willing to do for the right motivation."

She rolled her eyes, but her smile betrayed her amusement. "Well, I have to admit—you're pretty good at this."

"Don't sound so surprised," he teased.

The Finished Nook

When the project was finally complete, the transformation was stunning. The nook was everything Lila had imagined: a warm, inviting space with floor-to-ceiling shelves filled with her favorite books, a cushioned window seat bathed in soft natural light, and a small side table for her tea.

Lila stood in the doorway, her hand covering her mouth as she took it all in. "Ethan, this is... perfect."

He stood beside her, his hands tucked into his pockets. "I'm glad you like it. You deserve a space that feels like yours."

Lila turned to him, her eyes brimming with emotion. "This is more than just a nook. It's... it's you showing me that you care. That you're willing to put in the effort to make this work."

Ethan reached out, tucking a strand of hair behind her ear. "I'm all in, Lila. For this, for us—whatever it takes."

She leaned into him, her head resting against his chest. For the first time in a long time, she felt safe, like they were building something real and lasting.

A New Chapter

As they sat together in the finished nook later that evening, Lila with a book in hand and Ethan sipping coffee, the moment felt quiet yet profound.

"This feels like a new beginning," Lila said softly, glancing at Ethan.

"It is," he replied, his hand resting over hers. "And I can't wait to see where it takes us."

Chapter 9: Love in the Real World

The glow of reconciliation was warm and comforting, but as the weeks turned into months, Lila and Ethan began to navigate the complexities of building a life together. The joy of being in each other's orbit was undeniable, yet the challenges of integrating their lives while maintaining their individuality slowly came into focus.

Their love wasn't the idealized kind found in fairy tales; it was messy and imperfect. But it was real.

The Challenge of Balance

Despite their best efforts, moments of tension arose as Lila and Ethan adjusted to sharing their time and space.

Ethan had taken to spending more time at Lila's apartment, often working on his architectural sketches in her newly built reading nook. He found the space calming, almost inspiring, but his tendency to spread blueprints and models across her dining table became a point of contention.

"Ethan, I love that you're here," Lila said one evening as she tried to clear space for dinner. "But do you really need to use every surface for your projects?"

Ethan looked up sheepishly from a model he was assembling. "Sorry, I didn't even realize. I'll clean it up."

"It's not just about cleaning," Lila said gently. "I think we need to talk about boundaries—not just physical ones, but how we make room for each other without losing ourselves."

Ethan nodded thoughtfully. "You're right. I've been so focused on my work that I haven't thought about how it might be affecting you."

"And I know I can be a little particular about my space," Lila admitted, sitting down across from him. "But I want us to figure this out together."

They agreed to carve out intentional spaces for their respective pursuits—Ethan would create a dedicated workspace in his own apartment, and Lila would keep her reading nook as her sanctuary. It was a small compromise, but it felt significant.

Lila Sets Boundaries at Work

Lila had always been a hard worker, often staying late at the bookstore to organize events or finish tasks that weren't strictly her responsibility. But her relationship with Ethan made her realize how much of her personal life she had sacrificed for her job.

One evening, as she and Ethan shared takeout on her couch, she sighed and rubbed her temples.

"Long day?" Ethan asked, noticing her fatigue.

"More like a long week," Lila replied. "I've been covering shifts for a coworker, and I've barely had time to breathe."

Ethan frowned. "Lila, you're amazing at what you do, but you don't have to carry the entire store on your shoulders. Maybe it's time to set some boundaries."

Lila hesitated, the thought unfamiliar and uncomfortable. "I just don't want to let anyone down."

"Taking care of yourself isn't letting anyone down," Ethan said gently. "You deserve time for yourself—and for us."

The next day, Lila mustered the courage to speak with her manager. She explained that while she loved her job, she needed to prioritize her personal life and would no longer be able to cover extra shifts on short notice.

To her surprise, her manager was understanding. "Lila, you're one of the best employees we have," she said. "We'll make it work. Take the time you need."

The change was immediate. With more free time, Lila rediscovered hobbies she had neglected—painting, journaling, and even experimenting with new tea blends. She felt lighter, freer, and more present in her relationship with Ethan.

Ethan Rediscovers His Passion

Ethan's career in architecture had been a source of pride, but somewhere along the way, he had lost the spark that had drawn him to the field. His projects had become more about meeting deadlines and less about creativity. But being around Lila reignited something in him.

One afternoon, as he sat sketching in her reading nook, Lila noticed the wistful expression on his face.

"What's on your mind?" she asked, sitting beside him.

Ethan held up his sketch—a whimsical design for a small community library. "I don't know. Lately, I've been thinking about why I got into architecture in the first place. I wanted to create spaces that brought people together, that inspired them. But I feel like I've lost that somewhere along the way."

Lila studied the sketch, her eyes lighting up. "This is beautiful, Ethan. Why don't you pitch this to someone?"

He shook his head. "It's not practical. It's too small-scale. Most firms want big, flashy projects."

"Then find someone who values this kind of work," Lila said firmly. "You've got so much talent, Ethan. Don't let anyone tell you otherwise."

Her words stayed with him. Over the next few weeks, Ethan began reaching out to smaller firms and community organizations, sharing his designs and ideas. To his surprise, a local nonprofit expressed interest in funding one of his concepts—a mobile library that could bring books and resources to underserved neighborhoods.

When he told Lila the news, she threw her arms around him, beaming. "Ethan, that's amazing! I'm so proud of you."

For the first time in years, Ethan felt a renewed sense of purpose.

Celebrating the Small Moments

While their individual growth was fulfilling, it was the small, everyday moments that truly defined their relationship.

One Saturday morning, Lila woke to the smell of coffee and the sound of soft jazz playing in the background. She wandered into the kitchen to find Ethan standing at the stove, flipping pancakes.

"Good morning," he said, glancing over his shoulder with a smile.

"Good morning," Lila replied, leaning against the doorway. "What's all this?"

"I thought we could have a lazy breakfast," Ethan said, gesturing to the table, which was set with plates, syrup, and a small vase of daisies.

Lila's heart swelled. "You're spoiling me."

"You deserve it," Ethan said simply.

Later that evening, they curled up on the couch to watch a movie. Halfway through, Lila fell asleep with her head on Ethan's shoulder. He didn't mind; he muted the TV and sat there quietly, listening to her steady breathing and feeling grateful for the quiet intimacy they had built.

Finding Strength Together

Of course, not every moment was idyllic. There were disagreements, miscommunications, and times when old fears crept back in. But each challenge brought them closer, as they learned to navigate their differences with patience and understanding.

One evening, after a particularly stressful week, Ethan found himself snapping at Lila over something trivial.

"I didn't mean to leave the dishes," she said, her voice defensive. "I was rushing to finish a report."

"I'm not asking for perfection," Ethan said sharply. "I'm just asking for some consideration."

The room fell silent.

"I think we both need to cool off," Lila said finally, retreating to her reading nook.

An hour later, Ethan approached her, his expression contrite. "I'm sorry, Lila. I shouldn't have snapped at you. I was taking out my stress on you, and that wasn't fair."

She set down her book and looked at him. "I'm sorry too. I know I could've been more mindful."

They hugged, the tension melting away. Moments like these reminded them that love wasn't about avoiding conflict—it was about working through it together.

A Quiet Celebration

On their six-month anniversary of getting back together, Ethan surprised Lila with a handwritten note tucked inside her journal.

"Lila,

Six months ago, we decided to take small steps. Every step with you has been worth it. Thank you for believing in us.

Love,

Ethan"

Tears welled in her eyes as she read the note. That evening, she surprised him in return by cooking his favorite meal—homemade lasagna—and they shared it by candlelight in her living room.

As they clinked their glasses of wine, Lila smiled. "Here's to small steps—and big ones too."

Ethan chuckled. "And to love in the real world."

They had found their rhythm, imperfect but beautiful, and they knew they could face whatever came next together.

Epilogue: A Future Together

The bookstore hadn't changed much over the years. Its creaky wooden floors still groaned underfoot, the smell of old books mixed with fresh coffee still filled the air, and the faint murmur of customers browsing in hushed voices gave the space its familiar charm.

But for Lila and Ethan, it was more than just a store. It was the place where everything began—their first meeting, the spark of something neither of them could have predicted, and the long journey that brought them here today.

Years of Growth

It had been three years since that rainy afternoon when Ethan surprised Lila at the same bookstore. Since then, their lives had evolved in ways neither of them had imagined. They weren't just surviving; they were thriving—both as individuals and as a couple.

Lila had finally taken the leap to open her own small business: a cozy tea shop nestled in a quiet neighborhood, filled with shelves of books and local art. She had poured her heart into creating a space that reflected her passions, and it had quickly become a favorite spot for book lovers and tea enthusiasts alike.

Her success wasn't just in the numbers—it was in the way she felt every time she walked through the doors. The shop was her sanctuary, her creation, and a testament to the risks she had taken to prioritize her dreams.

Ethan, too, had found his footing. His decision to focus on smaller, community-centered projects had revitalized his passion for architecture. Over the years, he had designed libraries, schools, and even affordable housing complexes—spaces that fostered connection and served a purpose beyond aesthetics.

One of his proudest achievements was the mobile library he had pitched years ago, now a thriving initiative that brought books and resources to underserved areas. And through it all, Lila had been his biggest cheerleader, inspiring him with her unwavering belief in his talent.

Reflecting on Their Journey

As they strolled through the bookstore on a quiet Saturday morning, Lila reached for a copy of a newly released novel, running her fingers along the embossed cover.

"Do you remember the first time we met here?" she asked, glancing at Ethan with a playful smile.

Ethan chuckled, leaning against the edge of the shelf. "How could I forget? You almost dropped your coffee on me."

"That's not how I remember it," Lila said, feigning indignation. "You were the one who bumped into me, Mr. Oblivious."

"Fair enough," Ethan conceded with a grin. "But I'm pretty sure I redeemed myself when I bought you a replacement coffee."

Lila laughed, the sound warm and melodic. "You did. And I remember thinking, 'Who is this ridiculously awkward guy who just ruined my book and then tried to make it better?'"

Ethan tilted his head, pretending to think. "And I remember thinking, 'Who is this stubborn woman who won't let me help her carry her books but is clearly juggling too much at once?'"

They both laughed, the memory a cherished piece of their shared history.

Building a Life Together

Their relationship had grown stronger over the years, not because it was perfect, but because they had learned to navigate life's challenges as a team.

Ethan still spent hours tinkering with blueprints and models, but he had learned to balance his work with time spent with Lila. And Lila, while fiercely independent, had learned to let Ethan in when she needed support.

Their home—a light-filled apartment with floor-to-ceiling windows and walls lined with bookshelves—was a blend of their personalities. Ethan's sleek, minimalistic design sense complemented Lila's love for warm, cozy textures. The reading nook Ethan had built in her old apartment had been recreated here, a centerpiece of their shared space.

Saturday mornings were sacred to them. Lila would brew a pot of her latest tea blend, and they would curl up on the couch together, each lost in their own book. It was a simple ritual, but one that grounded them amidst the chaos of their busy lives.

A Sweet Moment

As they continued browsing the bookstore, Lila paused in front of a display table stacked with copies of "The Stars We Watch", the anthology that had brought them together all those years ago.

"Look at this," she said, picking up a copy and holding it out to Ethan.

He smiled, his eyes twinkling with recognition. "Still your favorite?"

"Always," she replied. "It's the reason we're here, isn't it?"

Ethan reached for the book, flipping through the pages. "Do you remember the story about the astronaut who gets lost in space but finds a way back home?"

Lila nodded, her gaze softening. "That one's my favorite. It's about finding hope, even in the darkest places."

Ethan closed the book and handed it back to her. "Kind of like us, isn't it? We lost each other for a while, but we found our way back."

Lila smiled, slipping the book back onto the shelf. "I guess we did."

Planning for the Future

Later, as they sat together in the bookstore café, Lila sipped her tea while Ethan sketched ideas for a new community project on a napkin.

"What are you working on now?" she asked, leaning over to get a better look.

"It's a park," Ethan said, his voice tinged with excitement. "A space for kids to play, for families to gather—something that brings people together."

Lila studied the sketch, her hand resting lightly on his arm. "I love it. It's exactly the kind of thing this city needs."

Ethan glanced at her, his expression soft. "You know, I couldn't have done any of this without you."

"Don't give me too much credit," Lila said with a laugh. "You've always had it in you. I just reminded you of that."

He reached for her hand, threading his fingers through hers. "Well, either way, I'm glad we're here—together."

A Full Circle

As they left the bookstore, the sun peeked through the clouds, casting a golden glow over the city streets. Lila slipped her arm through Ethan's, leaning into him as they walked.

"Do you ever think about how different our lives would be if we hadn't met that day?" she asked.

"All the time," Ethan admitted. "And every time, I feel grateful that we did."

They paused at the corner, the same spot where they had first crossed paths all those years ago. Ethan glanced at Lila, a playful glint in his eye.

"Want to grab a coffee? My treat," he said, echoing the words he had spoken the first day they met.

Lila laughed, swatting his arm lightly. "Only if you promise not to spill it on me this time."

"I make no promises," Ethan teased, pulling her closer.

As they stepped into the café, the door chimed behind them, signaling the start of another moment in their shared story—a story built on love, resilience, and the small, meaningful steps that had brought them to this point.

A Future of Possibilities

Years from now, they would look back on this day and smile, knowing that their love had been forged not in perfection but in perseverance. It was the kind of love that grew stronger with time, rooted in trust, laughter, and a shared commitment to building a future together.

For Lila and Ethan, the best chapters were still ahead.

Don't miss out!

Visit the website below and you can sign up to receive emails whenever MOSES MUTISO publishes a new book. There's no charge and no obligation.

https://books2read.com/r/B-A-QXBXC-TBQKF

BOOKS 2 READ

Connecting independent readers to independent writers.

Also by MOSES MUTISO

Embrace Your Size: A Guide to Managing Body Image and Health
The Fall from Grace: A Story of Manipulation in a Mega Church
Behind the Veil of Control The Tactics of Dark Lords
Beyond the Screen A Journey Toward Conscious Living
Embrace Your Size: A Guide to Managing Body Image and Health
Serendipity in the Stacks
Serendipity in the Stacks
Serendipity in the Stacks

www.ingramcontent.com/pod-product-compliance
Lightning Source LLC
LaVergne TN
LVHW010117170826
845678LV00012B/2463

* 9 7 9 8 2 3 0 4 9 1 5 0 7 *